PRINCE BERTRAM THE BAD

by ARNOLD LOBEL

Christy Ottaviano Books

Henry Holt and Company ✦ New York

To my grandparents

Henry Holt and Company, *Publishers since 1866*
Henry Holt® is a registered trademark of Macmillan Publishing Group, LLC
175 Fifth Avenue, New York, NY 10010 • mackids.com

Copyright © 1987 by the Estate of Arnold Lobel
All rights reserved.
First published in 1963 by Harper & Row Publishers
First Henry Holt edition, 2019

ISBN 978-1-250-14366-2
Library of Congress Control Number 2018963696

Our books may be purchased in bulk for promotional, educational, or business use.
Please contact your local bookseller or the Macmillan Corporate and Premium Sales Department
at (800) 221-7945 ext. 5442 or by e-mail at MacmillanSpecialMarkets@macmillan.com.

The artist used graphite, ink, and watercolor on paper
to create the illustrations for this book.
Printed in China by Toppan Leefung Printing Ltd.,
Dongguan City, Guangdong Province

10 9 8 7 6 5 4 3 2 1

A NOTE TO THE READER

I AM SO PLEASED that *Prince Bertram the Bad* is being made available to a new generation of children. It is one of my father's earliest books and also one of my favorites. Maybe that is because it was based on me! He wrote it when I was about five years old, and though Prince Bertram is a prince and not a princess, he looks (and acts) a lot like I did at that age.

My father was a warm and humorous man—and, yes—he did occasionally give me a spanking, but back then parenting discipline methods differed from those today. (He also spanked me gently and with such a mock-stern expression that it usually made me laugh, which did not help to discipline me at all.)

The comparison ends there as I never ran away from home and I was never turned into a dragon by a witch. That part comes from my father's wonderful imagination.

—Adrianne Lobel
2018

Once upon a time a prince was born.
"Long live Prince Bertram!" shouted all the
people in the kingdom.

   His mother and father, the king and queen,
were very happy and proud.

But Prince Bertram was not a good baby. In his crib
in the royal nursery he cried all the time.

When his mother took him to the park, Prince Bertram
was not friendly to the other babies.

Even before he was old enough to walk, he had torn up
all of the roses in the royal garden.

The king and queen hoped that Prince
Bertram would grow up to be a good boy. But as
each year passed, he grew meaner and naughtier.
He had a whole roomful of toys and he had
broken every one.

The royal coachman did not like Prince Bertram.
He would ride through the town blowing pebbles
at the people with his peashooter.

The royal cook would not speak to
Prince Bertram. He had thrown four
spiders into the chicken noodle soup.

The swans in the royal lake would not swim near
Prince Bertram. He made terrible noises and horrible
faces to frighten them.

"If only a spanking would do some good." The king
sighed. His hands were red and sore because he had to
spank Prince Bertram every day.

Of all the children in the whole kingdom
there was not one who was as mean and as nasty
as Prince Bertram. Everyone called him Prince
Bertram the Bad.

One morning
Prince Bertram
sat in the highest
castle tower
hitting the birds
with stones from
his slingshot.

He saw a large, long-nosed
black bird in the sky
and hit it, too.

It was not a long-nosed black bird at all but a witch,
who was passing by on her broomstick.

The witch was very angry with Prince Bertram.
She pointed a finger at him and shouted, "ALAGABIM."

Prince Bertram was quickly changed into a small scaly
dragon. "That will teach you to throw stones at me," said
the witch as she flew away.

"Mama, Papa . . . Help!"
called Prince Bertram.

The king and queen were startled.

"What has happened to our boy?" they cried.

Clouds of smoke and fire came out of Prince Bertram's mouth.

"What shall we do?" shouted the queen. "He will set fire to all
the window curtains!"

"That boy has been acting like a beast for so long that he has turned into a dragon," said all of the people in the kingdom. "There's nothing left of Prince Bertram but the crown on his head."

Everyone thought it was a great joke, and they came to the castle every day to laugh at him. Prince Bertram was tired of being laughed at. He was a very unhappy dragon.

One night he took some gingersnaps
from the royal pantry and ran away. There
was a big forest near the castle, where many
lions and porcupines and other beasts lived.
The animals growled and roared at him,
and they ate all of his gingersnaps.

The animals thought he was strange and no one
would play with him. Even the birds made fun of him.
Prince Bertram was lonely and sad.

Soon winter came. The wind grew cold, and the snow
began to fall. Prince Bertram tried to keep himself warm
with the fire from his breath. He wished that he were safely
home in the castle with his mother and father.

On the coldest day of the winter Prince Bertram was
walking through the forest, looking for something to eat.
Suddenly he saw two legs with shoes on them sticking
out of a snowbank.

Prince Bertram dug into the snow and was surprised
to find the very same witch who had changed him into
a dragon. She had lost her way while flying through a
snowstorm and had fallen, broomstick and all, into a deep
snowbank. Prince Bertram quickly opened his mouth and
blew a big breath of hot fire and smoke at her. The fire
melted the ice and the witch opened her eyes.

"You saved my life," said the witch. "Dear dragon, what is your name?"

"I used to be Prince Bertram until I threw a stone at you," said Prince Bertram sadly.

The witch remembered what she had done.

"Bless my broom," she said, "even witches make mistakes."

She pointed a finger and shouted, "ALAGABOOP!"

At once Prince Bertram was a boy again.

The witch flew Prince Bertram home,
and the king and queen were overjoyed
to see him.

The witch stayed for lunch.

Then she gave Prince Bertram and his mother and father
a ride on her broom.

As they flew over the kingdom the people cried, "Look,
Prince Bertram has come back, and he is no longer a beast."

That night at bedtime Prince Bertram heard
a voice outside his window.
"Good-bye, Bert, and stay well," said the witch.
Then she flew off into the evening sky.